HELLO, I'M THEA!

I'm *Geronimo Stilton*'s sister. As I'm sure you know from my brother's bestselling novels, I'm a special correspondent for *The Rodent's Gazette*, Mouse Island's most famous newspaper. Unlike my 'fraidy mouse brother, I absolutely adore traveling, having adventures, and meeting rodents from all around the world!

The adventure I want to tell you about begins at Mouseford Academy, the school I went to when I was a young mouseling. I had such a great experience there as a student that I came back to teach a journalism class.

When I returned as a grown mouse, I met five really special students: Colette, Nicky, Pamela, Paulina, and Violet. You could hardly imagine five more different mouselings, but they became great friends right away. And they liked me so much that they decided to name their group after me: the Thea Sisters! I was so touched by that, I decided to write about their adventures. So turn the page to read a fabumouse adventure about the

THEA SISTERS!

nicky

Name: Nicky
Nickname: Nic
Home: Australia
Secret ambition: Wants to be an ecologist.
Loves: Open spaces and nature.
Strengths: She is always in a good mood, as long as she's outdoors!

Weaknesses: She can't sit still!

Secret: Nicky is claustrophobic—she can't stand being in small, tight places.

Nicky

COLETTE

Name: Colette

Nickname: It's Colette, please. (She can't stand nicknames.)

Home: France

Secret ambition: Colette is very particular about her appearance. She wants to be a fashion writer.

Loves: The color pink.

Strengths: She's energetic and full of great ideas.

Weaknesses: She's always late!

Secret: To relax, there's nothing Colette likes more than a manicure and pedicure.

Colette

VIOLET

Name: Violet
Nickname: Vi
Home: China
Secret ambition: Wants to become a great violinist.
Loves: Books! She is a real intellectual, just like my brother, Geronimo.
Strengths: She's detail-oriented and always open to new things.
Weaknesses: She is a bit sensitive and can't stand being teased. And if she doesn't get enough sleep, she can be a real grouch!
Secret: She likes to unwind by listening to classical music and drinking green tea.

Violet

Name: Paulina
Nickname: Polly
Home: Peru
Secret ambition: Wants to be a scientist.
Loves: Traveling and meeting people from all over the world. She is also very close to her sister, Maria.
Strengths: Loves helping other rodents.
Weaknesses: She's shy and can be a bit clumsy.
Secret: She is a computer genius!

PAULINA

PAULINA

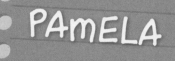

Name: Pamela
Nickname: Pam
Home: Tanzania
Secret ambition: Wants to become a sports journalist or a car mechanic.
Loves: Pizza, pizza, and more pizza! She'd eat pizza for breakfast if she could.
Strengths: She is a peacemaker. She can't stand arguments.
Weaknesses: She is very impulsive.
Secret: Give her a screwdriver and any mechanical problem will be solved!

Pamela

Geronimo Stilton

Thea Stilton
AND THE CHOCOLATE SABOTAGE

Scholastic Inc.

No part of this publication may be reproduced, stored in a retrieval system, or transmitted in any form or by any means, electronic, mechanical, photocopying, recording, or otherwise without written permission from the copyright holder. For information regarding permission, please contact: Atlantyca S.p.A., Via Leopardi 8, 20123 Milan, Italy; e-mail foreignrights@atlantyca.it, www.atlantyca.com.

ISBN 978-0-545-64656-7

Copyright © 2013 by Edizioni Piemme S.p.A., Corso Como 15, 20154 Milan, Italy.

International Rights © Atlantyca S.p.A.

English translation © 2014 by Atlantyca S.p.A.

GERONIMO STILTON and THEA STILTON names, characters, and related indicia are copyright, trademark, and exclusive license of Atlantyca S.p.A. All rights reserved. The moral right of the author has been asserted.

Based on an original idea by Elisabetta Dami.

www.geronimostilton.com

Published by Scholastic Inc., 557 Broadway, New York, NY 10012. SCHOLASTIC and associated logos are trademarks and/or registered trademarks of Scholastic Inc.

Stilton is the name of a famous English cheese. It is a registered trademark of the Stilton Cheese Makers' Association. For more information, go to www.stiltoncheese.com.

Text by Thea Stilton
Original title *Una cascata di cioccolato!*
Cover by Giuseppe Facciotto (design) and Flavio Ferron (color)
Illustrations by Chiara Balleello (design) and Daniele Verzini (color)
Graphics by Chiara Cebraro

Special thanks to Beth Dunfey
Translated by Emily Clement
Interior design by Kay Petronio

12 11 10 9 8 7 6 5 4 3 2 1   14 15 16 17 18 19/0

Printed in the U.S.A.   40
First printing, June 2014

THE SMELL OF ADVENTURE!

It was a beautiful morning when my ferry docked on Whale Island. I was greeted by a strong sea *breeze* and the eager, high-pitched squeak of **Mercury Whale**, the island's mailmouse.

"Miss Thea!" he shouted, STRETCHING a paw above the crowd. "Wait for me! I'm comiiiiiing!"

I *waved* back. A moment later, he'd scampered through the pack and reached my side.

"The headmaster asked

Welcome!

me to **piCK yoU uP**," Mercury explained. "He's **EXCITED** to see you!"

"I'm looking forward to seeing him, too," I said.

We clambered into Mercury's **VAN**, and soon we were speeding toward Mouseford Academy, where I studied as a young **moUSeLet**. Nowadays I return from time to time to teach **journalism** classes to a new crop of students.

Oh, pardon me, I almost forgot to introduce myself! My name is Thea Stilton, and I am special correspondent for *The Rodent's Gazette*, New Mouse City's **BIGGEST** newspaper. I was back at Mouseford to visit the headmaster, Octavius de Mousus, an old friend of mine.

As soon as we got to the academy, I sniffed the air. The smell of **chocolate** was overpowering!

"Where is that amazing aroma coming from?" Mercury exclaimed.

I smiled. "I think I know!" I thanked him for the ride and scurried down the hall to Professor de Mousus's office.

Before I could knock, the headmaster flung open the door and threw his paws around me. "My dear Thea!" he exclaimed. "Come in. I have a **SURPRISE** for you!"

Waiting for us on the coffee table were two cups of **hot chocolate**. "I see that the Thea Sisters sent you a special present from their most recent adventure!" I said. Colette, Nicky, PAMELA, PAULINA, and **Violet** — the THEA SISTERS — were the star students of my journalism class.

"Yes, indeed!" he replied. "This chocolate was shipped directly from Ecuador. Have you heard anything about their trip?"

"Yes," I said, booting up my **laptop**. "The mouselets sent me a long email and lots of **photos**. Make yourself comfortable, because I've got quite a tale to tell you! The **STORY** begins about a month ago, when Pam was feeling hungry one evening. . . ."

STUDiES AND SURPRiSES

It was a peaceful **EVENING** at Mouseford Academy. Almost all the students had retired to their dorm rooms. Only one doorway was still filled with **light**. Quiet chattering came from inside.

It was Nicky and Paulina's **ROOM**. The Thea Sisters were there, going over formulas for their math **test** the next day.

"I've got it!" Pam cried. "The answer to number five is thirty-six point nine!"

Nicky **LOOKED** up from her notebook. "But I got . . . seven."

"Me too," Colette said.

"So did we," Paulina and Violet added.

"Oh, crusty carburetors," Pam

sighed. "Sisters, I'm stuck. Solving these **problems** is harder than finding a cheese slice in a haystack!"

Colette gave her a pat on the head. "Don't despair, Pam. Let's go over it together."

Pam **beamed** at her. "I know just what we need — brain food! Let's try this snack I picked up today."

She **rummaged** through her backpack.

"Here we go. This will put us in a better mood." She held out a box of **chocolates**. "I wanted to eat them tomorrow after the test, but you know my motto: 'Never leave for tomorrow what you can eat today'!"

Nicky reached a **PAW** into the box. "According to some **STUDIES**, chocolate improves your concentration."

Paulina bit one in half. "**Mmm** . . . they're whisker-licking good!" she said. She glanced at the foil package. "Hey — that name . . . Pam, will you pass me the box?"

Her FRiEND did as she asked. "What are you looking for? The ingredients? No worries! They're very **high** quality —"

Paulina cut her off with a triumphant **SQUEAK**. "Antonio de Moreno . . .

Quito . . . It must be him!"

"Him who?" asked Colette.

"**Antonio** is an old school friend of mine," Paulina explained. "We were close when I lived in Peru, but we lost touch. He always *dreamed* of returning to his hometown, Quito, in Ecuador, and opening a **chocolate** factory! And look — **Cocoa Loco**, the company that made these delicious chocolates, is located in Quito, and its owner is **Antonio de Moreno**!"

It must be him!

"I guess Antonio made his **dream** come true," Nicky said.

"Yeah . . . I wish I could contact him," PAULINA replied. She went over to her **laptop**. "Who knows, maybe I can **find** him on SnoutBook." A moment later, she cried, "There! I found his email address!"

"**Write** to him!" Nicky suggested.

"Oh, but it's been so many years now," Paulina said. "He probably doesn't remember me. . . ."

"I'll bet he does," Pam said. "True friends never forget! *Go on, write to him!*"

Paulina smiled shyly. "Maybe I will."

The next morning, after the math test, the **mouselets** met outside the classroom and headed back to their dorm. They didn't know that a big *surprise* was in store for them.

There was an **email** alert waiting on Paulina's computer. "It's from Antonio!" Paulina cried. "He replied!"

"So you took our advice and emailed him," said Nicky.

"Does he *remember* you?" Pam asked.

"Yes, and he's written all about what he's been doing the last few years, and . . . mouselets, *you won't believe it!*" Paulina exclaimed. "Antonio has invited us to visit his factory!"

"*Sizzling spark plugs!*" Pam cried. "Now *my* dream will finally come true!"

"What *dream* are you talking about, Pam?" Violet asked.

Pam **winked** at her friends. "Why, my dream of becoming a professional **chocolate taste-tester**, of course!"

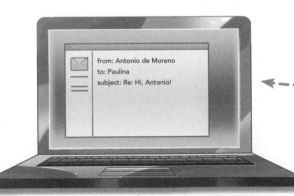

from: Antonio de Moreno
to: Paulina
subject: Re: Hi, Antonio!

THE KiNG OF CHOCOLATE

A few weeks later, Colette, Nicky, Pam, Paulina, and Violet were seated on a **PATIO** surrounded by banana plants. Each mouselet was sipping a tasty cup of **hot chocolate**. They had decided to accept **Antonio's** invitation, and they'd hopped on a flight to **Ecuador** the moment they'd finished their exams.

Antonio had picked them up from the airport in Quito, the country's capital, and driven them to the **small** village where he lived. He and his cousin Hector shared a quaint WOODEN cottage surrounded by trees.

The Thea Sisters had settled into a small guesthouse next door. After they'd unpacked their bags, they'd joined **Antonio** on the patio. He and Paulina were chatting about their mouseling days.

"Do you remember the first day of kindergarten?" Paulina asked. "You and your family had just moved to Peru from **Ecuador** and didn't know anyone."

Antonio smiled. "It's true, I was more nervous than a rodent in a lion's den! I had no idea where to go or what to do. If you hadn't shown up and taken me by the **PAW**, I'd still be lost. . . ."

Paulina laughed. "You were such a funny mouseling. And look at what you've done since then, Antonio! You've made your dreams come true."

"It's all thanks to my cousin Hector," the ratlet explained. "I can't wait for you to meet him! He was the **FIRST** to believe in the

chocolate factory. It wasn't easy in the beginning. You see, I wanted to build a modern business, but I also wanted to respect NATURE and eliminate the use of pesticides* on our cacao beans. For a long time, it looked like our dreams would be derailed by thousands of little PROBLEMS. But with the help of the rodents who work with us, we did it! And now we're in the running for the CHOCOLATE CUP award."

"An award?" Nicky asked. "What's it for?"

"Each year, a **jury** of experts from all over the world meets in Ecuador and votes on the highest-quality chocolate made in the country," Antonio explained. "Cocoa Loco's special DARK BARK BAR was selected for the competition."

"Dark Bark Bar? Sounds like a hangout for **dogs**!" Pam exclaimed.

---

* Pesticides are chemical substances that are used to eliminate pests that attack crops.

Antonio laughed. "No, no, it's our finest, most sophisticated **chocolate**, with a taste that can sometimes be a bit bitter. . . . Well, words don't really do it justice. Here, try it!" He took a chocolate bar in a **gold wrapper** out of his backpack.

The mouselets, curious, each took a small piece.

"**CRISPY CHEESE CHUNKS**, now *that's* what I call chocolate. It's so good you should call it the King of Chocolate!" Pam exclaimed.

"It's really delicious," Violet said. "You're going to win for sure."

"We hope so," Antonio said. "But now let's go to **Cocoa Loco**. Hector is expecting us. He's going to lead you on a tour of the factory and the *plantation*."

Paulina, Colette, Nicky, and Violet followed him. But Pam turned back to grab one last square of the DARK BARK BAR.

"Pam, what are you doing?" Paulina asked.

"I just can't leave behind a piece of that MARVEMOUSE chocolate," her friend replied. "If Antonio's competition finds it, they'll steal it and try to copy the recipe!"

"Good thing you know how to make the samples **disappear**, right?" said Paulina, winking.

Yum!

THE STRENGTH
OF A DREAM

Half an hour later, Antonio parked his **SUV** in front of **Cocoa Loco's** headquarters. It was a large, airy building with a bright sun shining down from its sign.

As they scrambled out of the car, the Thea Sisters noticed a dirt path running alongside the building. It led toward a field of low TREES full of orange fruit.

Curious, Colette approached one of the plants. Just as she was going to ask what they were, a deep **squeak** behind her explained, "Those are cacao plants, but they're not fully grown yet."

Turning, Colette found herself snout-to-snout with a mouse with **DARK** fur and bright eyes.

"Hi, I'm HECTOR, Antonio's cousin," he said. "These are the cacao fields that belong to our company." He leaned closer to the trees as he explained, "These plants are a very SPECIAL variety our grandfather Imasu gave us. He grew them for years in a hilly, volcanic part of Ecuador. We have some

It's a cacao plant!

plantations there."

Hector plucked a large orange fruit from the tree and used a small tool to crack it open. Inside, there were dozens of seeds. "These are the cacao beans we use to make all our products."

"From those tiny seeds you get something as **delicious** as this?" Pam asked, showing him the DARK BARK BAR's wrapper.

"That's right!" Antonio replied. "But it takes a lot of work. Come on, I'll show you."

The mouselets **FOLLOWED** their friends into the factory. They listened in awe as Antonio and Hector *eagerly* explained the process of transforming beans into chocolate.

"First of all," HECTOR began, "the beans are collected into large wooden boxes covered with banana leaves. We leave them to

FERMENT for five to seven days. This is when the seeds develop their distinctive **smell**."

"Then the seeds are left out to dry," Antonio continued.

The mouselets passed a group of rodents **pouring** the cacao beans onto large wooden tables.

Antonio invited the **mouselets** inside a building full of machines that looked like ovens. "Here the seeds are opened, toasted, and finally, ground into cacao powder. But we don't want to spill all our secrets on your first day, so we'll show you that process tomorrow." He smiled **PROUDLY**. "Our grandfather taught Hector and me to respect nature and tradition. We do everything using traditional methods."

"Cheese niblets!" Pam exclaimed. "I can see why you rodents are in the running for the **CHOCOLATE CUP** award! This place is amazing."

An Accident and
A Discovery

That night, the Thea Sisters all dreamed about **chocolate**. In Colette's dream, she invented a fabumouse chocolate-scented **perfume**. Violet listened to a string quartet whose instruments were made of chocolate, which the musicians devoured at the end of their performance.

Paulina and her **sister**, Maria, were making chocolate together. Nicky went **racing** through an immense cacao field. As for Pam, she **baked** the world's biggest chocolate cake!

After such sweet sleep, the mouselets woke up in **great** moods.

"I bet we'll get to **TASTE** some freshly made **chocolate** today," Pam exclaimed.

Antonio had promised they could help make the Dark Bark Bar, the bitter chocolate they'd enjoyed the day before. But the only thing bitter waiting for them at **Cocoa Loco** was the expression on Antonio's snout.

"Good morning, mouselets," he greeted them. "Unfortunately, we need to change our plans for today."

"What's wrong?" Paulina asked.

"We found a bunch of **FRUIT** in one of

the tanks of pure chocolate," Antonio said. "We don't know how it happened."

"Moldy mozzarella!" Pam exclaimed. "Did the fruit **RUIN** the chocolate?!"

Antonio sighed. "I think so. Adding an unexpected ingredient will definitely **ALTER** its taste."

"We'll have to throw away gallons of **chocolate**," said Hector, joining them.

"We certainly didn't need this just when we were a whisker away from **WINNING** an important award!" his cousin added.

"Do you have any idea how it happened?" Violet asked.

"Nope, no idea. Probably a crate that was supposed to contain cocoa butter was filled

with **fruit** instead," Antonio replied.

"Could someone who works here make that kind of **mistake**?" Violet asked.

"I don't think so," Hector replied, shaking his snout. "It seems like more than just carelessness. The CONSEQUENCES will be **terrible**!"

"Did someone break into the factory last night?" Nicky asked.

It's a mess!

"No," Antonio said with certainty. "**No one** would do something like that!"

Hector placed a paw on his shoulder. "Actually, Antonio, I think someone —"

He was interrupted by a loud shriek from inside the factory.

"AAAAAAAAH!"

"PAM!" the Thea Sisters shouted together, recognizing their friend's squeak.

Colette, Nicky, Paulina, Violet, Hector, and Antonio rushed onto the factory floor. The smell of chocolate was exhilarating, but the mouselets scarcely noticed.

"She's over there!" Paulina shouted, pointing to a curly head of fur poking out from behind a large vat.

"Pam! What happened?" Violet asked.

"Are you okay?!" said Nicky.

"I'm great, sisters," said Pam, licking something off her paws. "I just got a little too close to the **chocolate** vat — I almost fell in."

"You SCARED us!" Colette gasped. "But . . . what are you eating?"

"It's a piece of Indian fig. I just tried it, and

it's **delicious**, especially covered in melted chocolate!"

"Really?" Antonio asked. "I thought the fruit had **Ruined** the chocolate!"

"Maybe not," Paulina said. "This is so good. . . . No, scratch that. It's **GREAT**!"

"Here's some banana. . . ." Antonio said, pulling out a piece covered in **chocolate**.

Hector glanced over at the Thea Sisters. By now, they were all pulling pieces of fruit out of the vat and **TASTING** them. "Um, mouselets?"

No one noticed. They were all too busy eating.

"**MOUSELETS!**" he exclaimed.

Everyone turned to look at him.

"What's up?" Antonio asked.

"I have an **idea**! Well, it was really Pam's idea. . . ."

"Me?!" the mouselet asked, $savoring$ a piecc of chocolate-covered pear.

Hector nodded. "It's the next new product from **Cocoa Loco**: dark chocolate–covered fruit!"

A NEW PROBLEM

Thanks to Pam's appetite and Hector's **brainstorm**, the fruit accident had inspired a new product! Antonio and Hector got to work immediately, while the mouselets decided to take in the wonders of **Ecuador**.

"I wish I could go with you, but the **COMPANY** needs me right now," Antonio apologized.

"Don't worry your busy little snout about us. We're **expert** tourists," Paulina said. "Right, mouselets?"

Colette, Nicky, Pam, and Violet **AGREED** enthusiastically. The five mice headed over to the patio to look through their guidebooks and decide on the day's destination.

"From **Quito** we can go on lots of different

day trips," Violet said. "The Cotopaxi volcano sounds pretty interesting. . . ."

"But look, it's so close to Cocoa Loco's most important PLANTATIONS. Antonio said that he would take us to **visit** them in a day or two, and we could see Cotopaxi then," Nicky said.

Let's go here!

"Good point, Nicky. Okay, so we could visit Quito . . . or Otavalo, a city known for its **CLOTH MARKET**," Violet replied.

"Cloth market?" Colette squealed, her eyes **shining**. "That sounds awesome! Ecuador is famouse for its **fabrics**. We could make our own purses and **clothes**!"

"It's decided, then," Pam said.

THE REPUBLIC OF ECUADOR

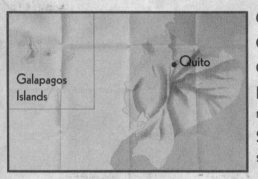

Capital: Quito

Government: Republic

Official language: Spanish

Population: More than 15 million people

Surface Area: 98,985 square miles

ECUADOR is located in the northwestern region of South America, on the coast of the Pacific Ocean. Its name comes from the fact that the country is located on the equator, which runs through the capital of Quito.

Ecuador includes the **GALAPAGOS ISLANDS**, which

are more than six hundred miles from the coastline. The islands are known for the countless plant and animal species that live there, including a famous species of turtle.

THE FLAG of Ecuador has three colors, and each represents part of the country's heritage. Yellow stands for the fertility of the crops and land, blue for the ocean and the sky, and red for

the lives that Ecuador's patriots have spent for their country.

"Are you sure, **mouselets**? I don't want to drag you along if you're not that into it," Colette said.

"Oh, it's no problem, Colette. As long as you promise to make purses for **everyone**!" Violet joked.

Three hours later, the Thea Sisters were wandering through the **BOOTHS** of the Otavalo market.

"These fabrics are woven by paw. Aren't they gorgeous?" Violet noted as Colette admired some colorful **necklaces** and earrings.

"How do I **LOOK**?" Paulina asked, trying on a big **STRIPED** hat.

Soon each **mouselet** had found a corner of the market that seemed made especially

OTAVALO is Ecuador's best-known market town. It's famous for its cotton and woolen fabrics, which are handwoven by local artisans. The Saturday market also offers a vast selection of rugs, jewelry, and other handicrafts.

for her. The hours passed in a FLASH.

That evening, the Thea Sisters returned home loaded down with packages. A **NOTE** from Antonio was waiting for them:

Hi, mouselets,

We'll see you tomorrow morning at the factory for the tour we promised. Get ready to learn all about how we make our chocolate bars!

Antonio

"**Hooray!** I can't wait!" Paulina exclaimed, jumping into bed.

The next morning, the mouselets woke up early and **EXCITED**.

Hector and Antonio met them on the street

in front of the factory. Both ratlets were **smiling** broadly.

"Yesterday we spent the day thinking about our new **SPECIALTY**: chocolate-covered fruit," Antonio said. "We decided to call the bars **Pam's Chocolate Surprise**, in honor of the friend who helped us realize that a problem was just an opportunity in disguise!"

Pam's Chocolate Surprise!

"There's going to be a chocolate bar with my **NAME** on it?" Pam asked incredulously. "This is the **best day ever**!"

Hector grinned at her. "Now **let's go**. We promised you a tour!"

But when they reached the **factory**

gates, the two cousins stopped.

"That's weird," Antonio murmured. "The gate is **already open**!"

"Look! Someone's running away!" Hector exclaimed, **POINTING** to a figure hurrying away from the **chocolate** factory.

A CHASE!

Hector **RACED** after the mystery rodent. In just a few steps, he'd **Reached** the fleeing figure. "Stop! Now tell me **what** you were doing inside our factory. . . ."

But when Hector **SAW** the rodent's snout, he stopped in shock. **"YOU?!"**

"Luz?!" said Antonio, who had **CAUGHT** up to them. "What in the name of cheddar are you doing here?"

"Yeah!" Hector said.

You?!

His squeak had turned icy. "Why were you sneaking into our factory?"

"I . . ." the mouselet began, lowering her eyes. "I just wanted to . . ."

"What?" Hector snapped. "Oh, I'll bet I know! You wanted to play another trick, like with the fruit, right?"

Luz raised her EYES to his snout. She looked HURt. "What trick? Do you really think I'm here to do something bad?" She shook her snout. "You're the same as always, Hector! You never listen."

Colette realized that the mouselet was hiding something behind her back. But before she could alert the others, Luz managed to wiggle out of Hector's grasp. A moment later, she'd darted away and DISAPPEARED from view.

The Thea Sisters surrounded

Hector, who was clearly **distressed** by the encounter.

"Who was that mouselet?" Nicky asked.

Hector's **EXPRESSION** darkened.

"No one!" he said sourly. "It was no one! And now excuse me, but I need to **CHECK** and see if some terrible surprise is waiting for us inside the **FACTORY**."

He **stormed** away.

Antonio **STEPPED** forward. "Don't mind him, he's just upset."

"So you **KNOW** that **mouselet**. We can see she and Hector have a history," Colette said.

It was no one!

"Yes," Antonio **SIGHED**, sinking onto a nearby bench. "The story is longer than a cat's tail. Come have a seat and I'll tell you about it. . . ."

THE STORY OF LUZ

The Thea Sisters gathered around Antonio, eager to hear the story of this mysterious mouselet.

Their friend took a deep breath and began. "HECTOR and Luz have known each other since they were little mouselings, and they've always been close. They studied together and spent all their free time side by side. Even when they were little mice, they had big dreams for their future. They squabbled constantly — they're both more stubborn than shrewmice. But it was obvious to everyone that theirs was a deep and sincere friendship."

"Then what happened?" Colette asked. "Hector seemed so angry."

"**HE iS**," Antonio admitted. "Everything changed two years ago, when we decided to found **Cocoa Loco**. Luz was really excited about the idea, and she helped us start the business. We all worked together on the **renovation** of the factory and the development of the plantations. The business was already up and **RUNNING**. We were frantically busy trying to fulfill orders from the most important shops in Quito. And then, suddenly, Luz left."

"What?!" exclaimed Pam.

"Where did she go?" asked Paulina.

"And why?" wondered Colette.

"What did she say?" said Nicky.

"MOUSELETS!" interrupted Violet. "One question at a time! Let's give Antonio a chance to answer."

The ratlet smiled gratefully at Violet. "Luz left without an explanation, and she went to work for ChocoMax!"

"ChocoMax?" Paulina said. "I saw some billboards for a company with that name in Otavalo. They make chocolate, right?"

"That's right," Antonio said. "It's the biggest chocolate company in this area."

"So they're your COMPETITION?" Paulina guessed.

"Yes, but that's not all," Antonio replied. "The fact is, ChocoMax is only **INTERESTED** in money. They use **PESTICIDES**  and farming methods that are very harsh on the environment. They pay no attention to the earth's natural cycles."

"That's the complete opposite of your **philosophy** and production methods!" Colette exclaimed.

Antonio nodded. "Yes. You can understand why that hurt Hector."

"**GREASY CAT GUTS**, that's terrible!" Pam said.

The mouselets exchanged a look of concern. How was it possible for a **FRIENDSHIP** like Hector and Luz's to end so suddenly, and seemingly for no reason?

"And Luz never gave you an **EXPLANATION**?" Violet asked.

"No, never. All I know is that, some time later, Hector tried to squeak with her, but she was **colder** than iced cheese toward him. He said she acted as if he were a stranger. So Hector decided to never mention her again, and to behave as though **Luz** had never been a part of his life."

Colette let out a big **sigh**. "What a sad story!"

"You're right, Colette, it is **SAD**, especially when you're here to enjoy yourselves," agreed Antonio, shaking off his glum mood. "Come on, let's go. I promised you'd help us make the **DARK BARK BAR** — the King of Chocolate is waiting for you!"

Antonio got up and led the Thea Sisters toward the **factory**.

As she followed Antonio, Colette couldn't stop thinking about the story of Hector and Luz. She wondered if there might be a way to make PEACE between the two former friends. . . .

A SECOND ACCIDENT

All day long, Colette was as **PREOCCUPIED** as a kitten with a new ball of yarn. She couldn't stop thinking about the story Antonio had told them. She was still brooding about it when she fell asleep that night.

In the **morning**, the hot, bright sun greeted the Thea Sisters. Hector and Antonio had invited the mouselets onto the patio for a tasty **BREAKFAST**.

"Mmm . . . scrambled eggs, potatoes, fresh fruit, and corn tortillas! This is great," Nicky exclaimed, eyeing the food Antonio placed before her.

Pam was already seated at the table. She was **filling** her plate with small brown balls from a serving tray.

"What . . . **yawn** . . . are those?" asked Violet, who was a bit of a sleepysnout.

"I don't know," Pam replied, "but they smell **DELICIOUS!**"

Antonio laughed. "They're called *pan de yuca*, and they're little rolls made from **cheese** and tapioca flour. We eat them with yogurt," he explained, placing a jug **OVERFLOWING** with fresh yogurt and fruit on the table.

Between mouthfuls, the mouselets relaxed. The tension of the previous day seemed like a **bad memory**.

Hector seemed much calmer today. He was laughing and **joking** around with his new friends.

"So, mouselets, what are your plans for the

day? I'm sure you don't want to come back to the factory with us."

"Why, are we a **pain** in the tail?" Nicky asked, dismayed.

"Oh no, of course not!" Hector replied. "But it's such a BEAUTIFUL DAY. It would be a shame for you to be stuck inside. You should take a day trip."

Antonio agreed.

"**Ecuador** is full of wonders, and up till now you've only sampled the culinary ones."

"Good point, Antonio," Colette said, smiling. "Why don't you and Paulina put your snouts together and come up with a **PLAN** for the day? Meanwhile, the rest of us can go to **WORK** with Hector for a bit."

Paulina shot Colette a grateful **smile**. Since they'd

arrived, she hadn't managed to find a moment alone with her old friend. And they had so many things to **talk** about — so many stories to **TELL**!

Antonio weighed her suggestion. "That sounds great, but I have a lot of responsibilities today. . . ."

Hector reached out a paw and ruffled his **fur**. "Of course . . . like your responsibility as a host! The **mouselets** can come with me while you help Paulina **brainstorm** activities."

Half an hour later, Hector, Colette, Nicky, Pam, and Violet were outside the gates of Cocoa Loco.

Help Paulina!

"While we wait for Antonio and Paulina, we'll take a quick **tour** of the building," Hector said, leading them **inSide**. "I do it most mornings to make sure everything's **in order**."

Soon the Thea Sisters were immersed in the **ma gical** world of the chocolate factory once more. Together they scampered through the areas where the cacao beans were chosen, toasted, ground, **MELTED**, and finally transformed into delicious bars.

EVERYTHING seemed to be going like clockwork until Hector approached the toasting machine. There was a **worried** look on his snout.

"Is something **WRONG**?" Nicky asked, joining him.

"Yes!" the ratlet exclaimed. "The toaster is blocked."

"Rancid rat hairs! Let me take a look," said Pam, examining the machine. "There's

damage to the central wheel, the one that turns the beans. It's stuck."

Hector asked the machine operator to switch everything off. Then he shook his snout angrily. "We didn't need this! Today is Sunday and our **mechanic** isn't working. . . . I can't believe all these problems are just a coincidence."

Giving in to despair, he kicked a bag of cacao beans, which scattered everywhere.

Colette put a paw on his back. "Getting mad won't help anything. Snout up! You might not have your mechanic today, but we have ours."

Hector looked at her in surprise. Pam had already started taking apart the toaster, working with the sure movements of a rodent who knew exactly what she was doing.

"You're right, Hector. Your problems aren't

a coincidence. Someone has **SABOTAGED** your toaster!" she concluded.

"**I knew it!**" Hector exclaimed. "If only I could prove who it was. . . ."

"Do you have any **SUSPECTS**?" Nicky asked.

Hector opened his mouth to reply, but Pam cut him off. "We can think about that later! For now, bring me a pair of gloves and a **TOOLBOX**. Give me an hour, and I'll have the cacao beans toasting again."

This was sabotage!

SUSPECTS AND SQUABBLES

Meanwhile, Paulina and Antonio were on the patio, their snouts buried deep in Violet's **guidebook**. Once they'd figured out a plan, they started chattering, and time **flew by**.

So many things had happened during their years **apart**! After they'd spilled the first few secrets, stories and **laughter** started to flow like a **RIVER** of melted cheese.

Ha, ha, ha!

It was Antonio who realized that over an hour had gone by. It was past time they returned to **Cocoa Loco**.

When they reached the factory, everyone

was still busy with the **damaged** toaster. Luckily, Pam had managed to ⌈IX⌉ it, and production had started up again.

"I don't get it," Paulina commented after the others filled her in. "Which of your competitors could be so **mean**?"

"It's simple," Hector snapped. "There's only one rodent who turned her tail on us to **JOIN** the competition. But what I don't get is, **why now**? She never paid us any attention before —"

Antonio interrupted him. "Hector, you're not talking about —"

"Luz! That's right. She abandoned us when we were in **TROUBLE**, and now that we're successful, she's sticking her snout where it doesn't belong."

"**You can't be serious!**" Antonio replied. "Luz has always been our friend."

"Always? Do I have to remind you that she left us for **ChocoMax** without a squeak of explanation?"

"But that doesn't mean that she's the one who **sabotaged** our factory!" Antonio objected.

"That's exactly what it means. She's the one who put the **fruit** into our chocolate. We saw her running away, remember?"

"Yes, but I'm **sure** there's a logical

explanation," Antonio said. "Luz is not a bad rodent. We can't accuse her without any proof."

HECTOR chewed his whiskers. "If you think I'm being so unreasonable, then why don't you go sightsee today, too? I don't need you!"

Antonio stared at his cousin in disbelief. Then he spluttered, "What a load of goat cheese! If that's how you feel, then fine! I will!" He strode out of the FACTORY.

The Thea Sisters hurried after him. "Antonio, are you SURE you want to come with us?" Violet asked.

"Of course. You heard Hector, right? He doesn't need me. He wants me to get lost!"

The mouselets exchanged a LOOK. They needed to talk this through with Antonio, but he had to cool down first. Right now he was too angry to listen.

Half an hour later, when they arrived in **Quito's** Old Town, the Thea Sisters brought up the **ARGUMENT** again.

"You know, sometimes my little sister and I have huge **blowups**," Paulina began.

"I have lots of brothers," Pam put in. "We fight like cats and rats when we're all **TOGETHER**!"

"Even we mouselets squabble now and then," Nicky said.

"But **we love each other**," Violet added, "and when we're angry, we try not to say things we'll regret later."

"Because friends are **worth** their weight in Brie, even when they don't agree with you!" Colette concluded.

Antonio **LOOKED** at his new friends sadly. He was sorry he'd **left** his cousin alone.

"I can't believe I lost my cheese like that.

Hector is so **STUBBORN**." He sighed. "But that's one of the reasons he's so special! He's the best cousin in the world."

The Thea Sisters' work was done. Once **Antonio** had shown them how to find their way home, he returned to the factory to make peace with Hector.

"Hector has never resolved his quarrel with **Luz**. That's why he's **madder** than a cat with a bad case of fleas when she's around," Paulina said when they were alone again.

"Well, what do you say we help him **sort** things out?" Colette said.

The others stared at her in **shock**.

"Colette, you're crazy like a fox," said Nicky. "Simple but direct . . . I love it. *Let's do it!*"

The mouselets had a plan!

QUITO (San Francisco de Quito)

Villa de San Francisco de Quito, known simply as QUITO, is a vibrant city that stands at an altitude of 9,350 feet, making it the second-highest capital in the world (after La Paz, Bolivia).

Quito was founded in the 1500s on the ruins of an ancient city inhabited by the Incas. The city takes its name from an even more ancient people, the Quitu.

In 1978, Quito's Old Town was declared a UNESCO World Heritage Site for its beautiful architecture. The historic city center is home to forty churches, including the Church of San Francisco and its monastery. Construction on San Francisco began around 1550 and lasted for about 150 years. The church is considered an architectural jewel for its interior, which is covered with gilded and painted wood.

The Church of San Francisco

THE SEARCH FOR LUZ

Colette asked Paulina to look up Luz's address on her MousePad. Paulina found it almost immediately.

"I want to meet her and squeak with her," Colette explained. "I have a feeling her story is more complicated than Hector thinks. Plus, she may have seen something at the FACTORY the other day."

"I'll go with you," proposed Nicky, pulling out a BIG map. "You've got the best ideas, but you don't always have the best sense of direction. You're going to need a navigator."

Colette pouted for a minute, and then burst out LAUGHING. "I hate to admit it, but you're right! Besides, there's strength in numbers."

While the others **returned** to Cocoa Loco, Colette and Nicky hit the city *streets*. They **SCAMPERED** along till they reached **Luz's** neighborhood.

"Are we there yet?" Colette asked after half an hour's brisk walk. "My paws are getting a little sore."

"Come on, we've almost made it! It must be that one over there." Nicky pointed to a **dilapidated** house a few doors down.

We're almost there!

"Are you sure?" Colette asked. "It looks abandoned. . . ."

Just then, a shutter on the first floor **flew** open, nearly hitting Nicky on the snout. She quickly ducked out of the way.

"**Luz!**" said Colette, staring at

the mouselet in the window.

Luz was startled. "You . . . you're HECTOR'S friends! What are you doing here?"

"We came to squeak with you," Nicky replied.

"Oh, so you want to shout at me, too?" demanded Luz.

"No, we just want to ask you some questions about the Moreno cousins and Cocoa Loco," Colette replied.

"Why, did something happen?" Luz asked. She sounded ALARMED.

"Well, it seems like someone has been sabotaging their business," Nicky replied. "First some fruit was dumped into a vat of dark chocolate, and then someone TAMPERED with the toasting machine."

Luz looked at Colette and Nicky suspiciously. "And you're accusing me, is that right?"

"Not at all!" Colette exclaimed. "We know the story of your friendship with Hector, and we're sure that, in spite of the MISUNDERSTANDINGS, you still care about him."

Luz seemed surprised. She was about to say something, but then she just shook her snout. "It's all in the past. . . . Hector and I don't have anything to say to each other anymore."

Colette wasn't going to give up. "Are you sure? The other day, I saw you had an envelope. Was it a letter for him?"

"You're wrong. I didn't have an envelope," Luz replied.

"But that's what it looked like. . . ." Colette protested.

"I'm sorry, mouselets, but I don't have anything else to say," Luz concluded.

A voice from **INSIDE** called Luz's name.

"My mother needs me. Good-bye," Luz said, **_hurrying away_** from the window.

Nicky and Colette exchanged a confused look. A moment later, they heard **Luz's** mother say, "Who were you talking to, _morenita*_?"

"Friends of Hector's," the mouselet replied.

Her mother sighed. "Are you sure you don't want to **CLEAR** things up with him? After all, it's all **OUR FAULT**. I'm sorry you were forced to . . ."

At that point, her squeak faded away. The two rodents must have **moved** to another room.

Who is right about the envelope? Turn to page 41 to find out!

---

* In Spanish, _morenita_ means "little brunette." It's an affectionate nickname.

"Coco, did you really see an **envelope** in Luz's paw?" Nicky asked.

"Yes, I saw it," Colette confirmed. "And I'm pretty certain it was a **love letter**."

"A love letter?!" her friend repeated in surprise.

"A **DECLARATION** to Hector that Luz doesn't have the courage to make in the fur. You know me, Nicky. I'm never wrong about this kind of thing," Colette said with a wink.

"Maybe . . . but for those two, I think it might be **too late** for love!" Nicky said, shaking her snout.

Colette smiled. "It's never too late for true love, Nic! Come on, we'd better go meet the others at **Cocoa Loco**."

SURPRISE TRIP

After the long trek across Quito, Colette was exhausted. That night she fell asleep as soon as her snout hit the PILLOW.

The next morning, she hoped to relax on the patio for a while. But her **FRIENDS** had a different plan in mind.

"Wait . . . you want me to wear this **THING**? It's going to destroy my fur-do!" she complained as Nicky pawed her a **pink** bicycle helmet.

"It's an absolute **MUST** for mountain biking," Nicky replied. "And look, it even comes in your favorite color!"

"Wait, did you say **mountain biking**?!"

"Uh-huh. **Antonio** and **HECTOR** are taking us on a bicycle trip through the hills,"

Nicky explained, **GRINNING**. "Shake a tail — they're already waiting!"

Colette *sighed,* but she put on the helmet.

Outside, standing next to a bunch of state-of-the-art bicycles, were Antonio and Hector. "Ready, mouselets?"

"I sure am," Pam said. She had an enormouse backpack slung over her shoulder.

"Pam, what have you got in that thing?" Paulina asked.

"Just a **few** snacks: *pan de yuca*, tortillas, and plenty of water."

"Sounds like we'll have to stop and have a picnic," said Hector.

Soon everyone was on their bikes, heading into the countryside.

"This place is amazing!"

said Violet, enjoying the view.

"The path we're following will take us along the slopes of Pasochoa, an extinct **volcano**," Antonio told the mouselets. "You're going to love it!"

The Thea Sisters pedaled single file behind the two ratlets. They were so absorbed in the sights around them that they didn't realize how much time had passed until Antonio said, "Mouselets, what do you say we take a break? That spot over there looks perfect for a picnic."

"Yesss!" Pam cried enthusiastically.

A few minutes later, the group was seated on a large blanket, passing around *pan de yuca*.

"Hey, Paulina, don't **tickle** me!" cried Pam, waving her paws.

The other mouselets giggled.

"Pam, that's not Paulina tickling you," Hector said. "Looks like you've made a new **friend**!"

Pam turned around . . . and found herself snout-to-snout with a llama! The creature was **STARING** hungrily at their snacks.

"**Get out of here**, greedy!" Pam said, laughing. "These aren't for you!"

Hee, hee, hee!

THE LLAMA

The Llama

The llama is an animal in the CAMELIDAE family. It's closely related to the alpaca. Since ancient times, the people of Central and South America have DOMESTICATED llamas, using them to transport goods and shearing their precious wool for clothing. Llamas are strong and sure-footed, with easygoing temperaments.

Annoyed, the animal turned and **sashayed** away.

"Thanks for rescuing our picnic," said Paulina, winking. "At last we can **KICK** up our paws for a bit."

But Paulina was **WRONG**. Their picnic was interrupted again — this time by a ratlet pedaling hard on a red bicycle.

"**PEDRITO!**" Hector cried. He recognized the ratlet as a worker from **Cocoa Loco**.

"What's going on?"

"Mr. Hector . . . Mr. Antonio . . ." the ratlet said, **GASPING** from his ride up the mountain. "I came to find you as quickly as I could! There's an **EMERGENCY**. A

There's an emergency!

plague of **pesky insects** has invaded the southern plantation."

"What a **CAT-ASTROPHE**!" Antonio **exclaimed**. "That's our main plantation! And we need another accident like mold on fresh mozzarella. . . ."

"Another accident . . . or another case of **SABOTAGE**?" Hector spluttered.

Antonio took charge of the situation. "Paulina and I will go to the plantation to find out what happened. Hector, you head back to the **FACTORY** with the mouselets. We can't let **anything else** go wrong!"

PEST ALERT

Antonio and Paulina **_RACED_** along the path to the plantation. They pedaled in **SILENCE**, lost in their thoughts, until they spotted cacao plants in the distance.

"**WE'RE HERE!**" the ratlet cried.

A moment later, they'd **reached** an open field where some plantation workers were **gathered**. "Mr. Antonio!" one exclaimed. "Thank goodmouse you're here!"

"What happened?" Antonio asked.

"The situation is serious," another **farmer** said. He led Antonio and Paulina through the trees. "The plantation was **_suddenly_** attacked by insects that are devouring the leaves and fruit!"

The farmer pulled down a **leaf** and

showed them what the insects had done.

"There are hundreds of them," the farmer continued. "And they're **swarming** over every part of the plantation."

"Have you ever seen anything **like** this?" Paulina asked.

Antonio shook his snout. "I've seen small outbreaks before . . . but never such a large invasion!"

"So what do we do now?" the mouselet wondered.

The first **FARMER** stepped forward. "We must use a strong dose of pesticides. There's no other solution."

"No! Never," Antonio said firmly. "Our business uses only natural methods. I have **never** used such products, and I'm not about to start now."

"But what will we do?" asked the farmer. "We could lose the whole crop!"

Antonio was silent for a long moment. He didn't know what to do. Should he abandon organic agriculture*? Or risk

---

* Organic agriculture means farming that doesn't use chemicals and pesticides, and that doesn't damage the soil or the surrounding environment.

LOSING the crop and, maybe, the entire plantation?

The ratlet thought of all the time they had spent carefully cultivating these **plants**, following his grandfather Imasu's traditional methods. . . .

"Of course! I've got it!" Antonio said. He turned to Paulina. "The only rodent who can help us is Grandfather Imasu! We must go to him immediately!"

GRANDFATHER IMASU'S ADVICE

Grandfather Imasu lived in a valley at the foot of a **MOUNTAIN** not far away. Antonio and Paulina climbed back on their bikes and set off.

A strained **SILENCE** fell between the two, which Paulina finally broke with a question. "Antonio, do you **THINK** this is more **sabotage**?"

"I don't know what to think, Paulina," Antonio replied. "To be honest, this sudden **insect invasion** does seem suspicious to me, especially after all the other setbacks we've had recently. . . ."

"But do you agree with Hector? Do you think **LUZ** is involved?"

Antonio shook his snout. He looked **worried**. "If you had asked me a week ago, I would have said no . . . but after everything that's happened, I'm not certain of anything! Except that someone is determined to muck up our production and keep us from winning the **award**."

"How could they prevent you from winning?" Paulina asked.

"The **CHOCOLATE CUP** isn't just for the best chocolate, but for the **best company**,"

Antonio explained. "The jury will visit the factory and plantations before deciding the award. With all the **PROBLEMS** we've been experiencing lately, it's hard to see how we'd pass their inspection."

Paulina thought about what the award meant for her friend, who had invested so much energy and hard work into his dream. She tried to find the right words to make him understand she was there for him.

But before she could squeak, they had **ARRIVED** at a small stone cottage with a GARDEN out front. Antonio hopped off his bike and knocked on the door.

What a surprise!

A moment **LATER**, a **cheerful** old rodent appeared at the window.

"Grandfather Imasu!" Antonio cried, hugging him warmly.

His grandfather welcomed them into the house. The three

rodents sat down around the cozy kitchen table.

Antonio explained what had happened at the **plantation**, and Grandfather Imasu listened attentively.

Antonio showed his grandfather a leaf that had been eaten by the **insects**. "There must be something we can we do," he said anxiously. "Is using **pesticides** really the only remedy?"

Imasu *smiled*, grabbed his cap, and jumped to his paws. "My dear ratlet, sometimes nature causes problems . . . but it also supplies the SOLUTIONS. Come on!"

The elderly rodent led them into the **garden**, where he gathered some potatoes. "These are sweet potatoes, and they **repel**

insects. Scatter them throughout the cacao plants, and they'll drive away the little intruders. Then look for small holes in the stems of the PLaNtS. The insects bore these holes and use them as nests. If you seal them up with **SOAP**, your plantation will be saved!"

Antonio thanked his grandfather. Because of his **wisdom** they had found a good, ECOLOGICAL solution!

DESTINATION: CHOCOMAX!

Meanwhile, Hector and the other Thea Sisters had returned to **Cocoa Loco**.

"What bad luck! First all those accidents, and now an **insect infestation**!" Colette sighed.

Hector smiled bitterly. "Bad luck is when something goes **wrong**. We were sabotaged . . . and now I know who's **guilty**!"

The mouselets exchanged a worried look.

"Are you really sure it was **Luz**?" Violet asked.

"There's only way to know for certain. Follow me!" Hector said. He headed for the **van** Cocoa Loco used for deliveries.

Once inside the van, the mouselets were

enveloped in the DELICIOUS aroma of **chocolate**. The smell instantly comforted them.

"You'll see, we'll figure everything out," Colette told HECTOR, who was in the driver's seat.

But the ratlet didn't respond. He seemed lost in his thoughts, and gripped the wheel more **GLOOMILY** than a groundhog who's just seen his shadow.

The rest of the trip passed silently until they arrived at their **destination**.

"We're here," Hector said grimly.

"But . . . what are we **DOING** here?" asked Nicky. "This is —"

"**ChocoMax** headquarters!" cried Pam, pointing to the large glass-and-cement building in front of them. The sign for **Cocoa Loco's** main competitor sparkled in the sunshine.

Hector **marched** inside, with the **mouselets** trailing behind him.

"Hello. We're looking for Miss Luz Mendoza," he told the security guard at the front desk.

"Third floor, second office on the right," the guard replied without **raising** his snout.

Hector strode toward the elevator and pressed the UP button.

"I just can't believe Luz is involved in all these **ACCIDENTS**," Colette said.

"There's no other possibility," Hector replied. He **LOOKED** stern.

Colette didn't reply, but in her heart she was certain that Hector was wrong. His old friend just couldn't be the one trying to **sabotage** him.

When they arrived on the third floor, the ratlet knocked several times on Luz's office door, but no one responded.

Hector **threw** open the door. The room was empty.

"Are you looking for someone?" a **low** squeak croaked from behind them. An

unfriendly-looking rodent was staring at them from the end of the hallway.

"Yes, thank you. We'd like to know where we can find —" Colette began.

But then the rodent blurted, "**Moreno**? What are you doing here?"

"**ALVAREZ** . . ." Hector murmured. Turning to his friends, he added, "This is the owner of ChocoMax."

"Exactly," the other smirked. "You, on the other paw, are that crazy d**reamer** over at Cocoa Loco! Have you come to see how a real business is run?"

"What are you trying to say?!" cried Hector. "That my company isn't real?"

"Bah! Old methods, respect for this, respect for that . . . That's not how you do business, little ratlet!"

"Cocoa Loco has been **VERY** successful!"

Violet burst out in **irritation**.

"Don't listen to him, Vi. He's just trying to provoke Hector," Colette said. Then she turned to face Alvarez. "We're looking for **Luz Mendoza**."

"Ah yes, Mendoza. She's excellent, a very good worker. She hasn't come into the office for the last few days, though."

"Is she sick?" Nicky asked.

"How should I know?" Alvarez **SNIFFED**. "Maybe she's at home taking care of her family, or maybe she's on vacation. I can't keep track of all my employees!"

Ha, ha, ha!

"**Let's go**, sisters," Pam whispered. "This rodent is meaner than a hungry cat.

He's not going to help us."

HECTOR nodded. "We're leaving!" he said loudly.

"Good," Alvarez replied. "We have work to do here — not like at **Cocoa Loco**, where you have fun playing with fruit. What will your next invention be? **Chocolate-covered** insects? Ha, ha, ha!"

Hector started to reply, but Colette took him **GENTLY** by the paw. "Let's get out of here. We need to find **Luz**."

Did you notice anything suspicious about what Alvarez said?

COLETTE
INVESTIGATES

Once they were outside **ChocoMax**, the Thea Sisters and Hector paused to regroup.

"SLIMY SWISS CHEESE, what a loudmouth!" Pam spluttered.

"Yeah! Why in the world would Luz go **work** for him?" Nicky added. Then she noticed Hector's expression and changed the subject. "Anyway, we didn't DISCOVER anything useful."

"Maybe we didn't look hard enough," Colette said thoughtfully.

"What do you mean?" Hector asked.

"Well, if Luz had really come up with a plan to sabotage **Cocoa Loco**, she might have done research and taken notes on her computer."

"That's possible," Hector admitted. "But how can we find out?"

"Leave it to me," Colette said. "I saw something in the **VAN** that could be useful. Would you grab two **workmice** uniforms?"

A few minutes later, Colette and Nicky were dressed in gray **OVERaLLS**. They walked back into ChocoMax headquarters disguised as delivery mice. Each was carrying a large cardboard box.

"We need to take these boxes to the third floor," Colette said to the security guard. Distracted, as **before**, he pointed the mouselets toward the elevator.

"What's our **plan**?" Nicky asked as they went up. "I still don't quite understand what you want to do. . . ."

"You stand **guard** in the hallway while I look for information on the computer.

Alvarez mustn't see us!"

When they reached the third floor, Colette **SNUCK** into Luz's empty office and headed for the desk. Once she'd turned on the computer, she realized she'd need a **password** in order to access the files. "Oh no! What could it be?" she whispered.

A **SECOND** later, she heard pawsteps in the hallway. Colette ducked under the desk to hide, her **HeaRt** beating faster than

that of the mouse who ran up the clock.

Outside the door, Nicky spotted **Alvarez** coming down the hallway. She moved the **BOX** she was carrying a little higher to cover her snout.

Alvarez paused, and a chill went down Nicky's tail. She quickly squeezed into the nearest office, announcing, "I have a package to deliver!"

The rodent behind the desk gazed at her

A package?

over a set of thick **GLASSES**. "A package for me?"

"Actually, um . . . I have the **WRONG** floor, sorry!" Nicky apologized.

She PEERED out into the hallway. There was no sign of Alvarez. With a **sigh** of relief, she returned to her post outside Luz's office.

Colette was back on the computer, typing quickly. "Okay, **THINK, THINK, THINK** . . . most rodents choose a password that's close to their **HeaRt**. So if I were Luz . . ."

She quickly typed the word *morenita*, the nickname Luz's mother had used.

"**Access granted! Hooray!**" she cried, forgetting she was supposed to be sneaking around. "Oops." She scanned the computer screen and noticed a folder called "CL research."

"CL . . . as in **Cocoa Loco!**"

In the file there was lots of information on the Moreno cousins' business: a map of their **FACTORY**, plus notes on their chocolate-covered fruit, the toaster's mechanical trouble, and the insect invasion . . .

Colette couldn't believe it: All this **information** seemed to prove **Luz** was guilty! Was it possible that Colette's own instincts were **wrong**? It looked like Hector was right to doubt her.

The mouselet decided not to jump to conclusions and just made **note** of the useful information.

Colette was about to leave when she noticed a NOTEBOOK on the desk. She opened it and read the last note, which included an address.

There were **three** light knocks on the door — Nicky's signal that it was time to go.

Colette quickly made a note of the address, turned off the computer, and **hurried** away.

AT THE WAREHOUSE

Colette and Nicky scampered downstairs and joined the others, who were waiting next to the **van**.

"So, did you discover anything?" Hector asked **anxiously**.

"Well, um . . . there was a folder with information about **Cocoa Loco**. . . ."

"I knew it!" the ratlet burst out. "Isn't that what I've been squeaking all along?"

"Let's not **jump** to conclusions," Violet suggested. "Maybe there's an explanation."

"I hope so," Colette agreed. "I also **FOUND** this."

She showed her friends the address she'd written down.

"**Come on**, let's check it out," Hector

cried, scurrying into the van again.

The address belonged to an **abandoned** warehouse outside the city. Hector and the Thea Sisters explored the inside, which was huge and **dusty**. Tools were scattered in every corner. Nothing seemed to be in any kind of order.

"What a **strange** place," Nicky commented. "**WHAT** does it have to do with ChocoMax . . . or with Luz?" Violet wondered.

Suddenly, they heard a soft noise, like a sob, coming from the shadows.

"**Did you hear that?**" Colette asked.

"I didn't hear anything," Hector replied. "But I did find something."

The ratlet pointed to a pile of empty, dirty fruit **BOXES**, with pieces of **FRUIT** still splattered here and there.

"Hey! There's an old SUV over there, with

some strange **boxes** in it," Pam said.

Violet drew closer. "These boxes have tiny air holes. . . . They could have been used to transport **insects**!" She looked up at her friends. "This must be the SABOTEUR'S hideout!"

Just then, they all heard a noise from the back of the warehouse.

"Who's there? Come out!" Hector cried.

A rodent emerged from the SHADOWS with her snout down.

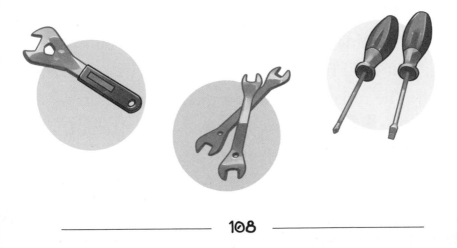

"**LUZ!** It *was* you!" Hector cried.

"That's not true, Hector!" the mouselet replied. Her fur was streaked with **TEARS**. "You don't know anything!"

"I know what I see: that you're here in your **hideout**, surrounded by tools you used to **SABOTAGE** us!"

"**STOP IT!**" Luz shouted. "You're so stubborn. Just because you found me here,

You don't know anything!

Those are all lies!

you think I must be GUILTY!"

"Well, then why are you here?" Violet asked.

"I was continuing my investigation," Luz began.

"Your investigation?!" asked Colette.

"Yes! A while ago, I REALIZED someone at ChocoMax was plotting against Cocoa Loco, and I've been trying to find out who —"

"Lies! All lies!" Hector burst out. "You abandoned us when we needed you, and now you want me to believe you're trying to help us?"

Luz smiled bitterly. "Hector, you never understood why I left Cocoa Loco. How could you? I never told you the whole truth. But now is the moment to do it."

LUZ'S CONFESSION

Luz lowered her **EYES**, as if she could find the rights words written on the warehouse floor. "I didn't want to **abandon** you. . . ." she finally whispered. "I was forced to."

"What do you mean? How?!" Hector **BLURTED**.

"Let her squeak," Violet said. "I think she has something **IMPORTANT** to say."

"You remember how difficult things were in the beginning," Luz continued. "We had just opened, and no one believed in us. Business wasn't going well."

This time, Hector just nodded.

"What I never told you was that my family was having serious financial TROUBLES. My mom and I were all alone, and when my

grandfather got sick, I . . . um . . . I had to . . ."

"Accept an offer from **ChocoMax**," Nicky filled in.

Luz nodded. "**Alvarez** needed an agronomist*, and I needed the money. I had to help my **family**."

"But why didn't you tell me?" Hector exclaimed in disbelief.

"Don't you understand? I was ashamed! You and your cousin were free to imagine your future and fight for your dreams, but I needed to think about my family first."

Silent **TEARS** ran down Luz's snout. Hector took a hesitant step toward her.

"Do you believe me now?" Luz asked him.

"I — I don't know what to think. All this time I was convinced that you left out of **selfishness**!"

Luz shook her snout. "It wasn't like that. I

---

* An agronomist is an expert in agriculture. She or he works to find new techniques for better farming.

had my reasons, but it was hard for me to explain them. I was too **proud** and you were too **stubborn**!"

"Well, when it comes to stubbornness, you mice have always been two of a kind!" **Antonio** broke in. He and Paulina had appeared on the warehouse's doorstep.

I had my reasons. . . .

"**_YOU'RE HERE!_**" Nicky exclaimed.

Paulina nodded. "Colette **texted** me with this address, and we rode our bikes over here. We've just gotten back from the plantation. Grandfather Isamu helped solve the **pest** problem."

"Well, over here we've solved a friend

Antonio! Paulina!

problem," Colette said, gesturing toward **HECTOR** and **Luz**. "These two have worked out a huge disagreement!"

Luz **SMILED** faintly. "I was finally able to explain everything."

"But we still have to figure out the mystery of the **SABOTAGE**," said Pam.

"Actually," Violet said, "I think I know who the culprit is!"

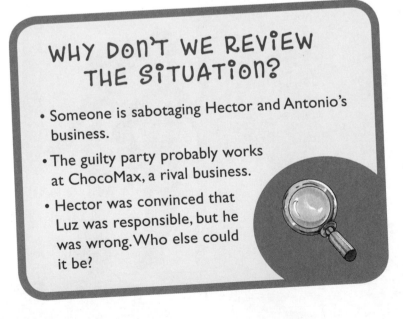

WHY DON'T WE REVIEW THE SITUATION?

- Someone is sabotaging Hector and Antonio's business.
- The guilty party probably works at ChocoMax, a rival business.
- Hector was convinced that Luz was responsible, but he was wrong. Who else could it be?

VIOLET'S
SUSPICIONS

Everyone turned to look at Violet.

"What do you mean, Vi?" asked Colette.

"First let's get out of this warehouse. Then I'll explain," Violet said.

The group scampered outside and gathered under the SHADE of a large tree.

"Let's think about it. Luz, you said that you suspected that someone from ChocoMax was plotting against Cocoa Loco, right?"

"Yes," the mouselet agreed. "I never got my paws on proof, but the accidents put me on alert. And since everyone at ChocoMax squeaks so enviously about the award being given to the Morenos, I figured someone inside the company was trying to sabotage them. My suspicions were confirmed when I **intercepted** a phone call in which **Cocoa Loco** was referred to as 'the target.' The caller mentioned the address of this warehouse."

Violet nodded. "I'm pretty sure the **GUILTY** rodent is someone at ChocoMax. But it's not Luz, like Hector thought. It's **Alvarez**!"

"What?" Antonio exclaimed. "How can you be sure?"

The target?

"Today we **VISITED** the ChocoMax offices, and we met him," Violet replied. "When he was talking to Hector, something he said didn't sound right to me, but I couldn't figure out what it was. Later, when I saw the **fruit** boxes, I understood!"

"Vi, are you sure? I'm not following you," Pam said.

Violet ꜱᴍɪled. "Don't you remember? Alvarez said that **Cocoa Loco** liked 'playing with fruit.' But how could he possibly know about the accident with the fruit in the **chocolate**? Only one rodent besides us would know about it . . . the one who arranged it!"

Don't you remember?

"Of course!" Luz said. "I remember hearing Alvarez order a load of fruit. It ꜱᴜʀᴘʀɪꜱed me because we don't use it in the factory."

The **Moreno** cousins were silent for a

moment. Antonio was the first to squeak. "Then everything was **the work of Alvarez!**"

"We should have realized it from the start," Hector added. "He's done nothing but get in our way since the very **first day** we opened!"

"And he stole away our **best** employee," Antonio said, placing a paw on **Luz's** shoulder. She smiled at him.

"It's all cheese under the wheel now," Colette concluded. "Now we've got to **CATCH** him in the act before he can cause any more damage!"

PAULINA'S PLAN

Pam stepped forward. "Come on! What are we waiting for? Let's go to the police and have them ARREST that greedy old cheddarface!"

She was striding toward the **van** when Colette's squeak stopped her. "Pam, wait! We can't do that. . . ."

"Why not?" Pam asked.

"COLETTE'S right," Nicky explained. "We don't have any **proof** of Alvarez's guilt. All we have are our suspicions."

"But we heard him talk about the fruit. Only the SABOTEUR would know about that!" Pam replied.

"Yes, but he can **deny** everything," Antonio said. "We need a witness, and no one else heard him besides you, did they?"

Colette **shook** her snout, disappointed.

But Pam wasn't ready to give in. "What about the **WAREHOUSE** and all the stuff in it? Isn't that enough **proof**?" she cried.

"I'm **AFRAID** not," Hector said. "Some empty fruit **crates** and a few tools don't prove anything."

"Rat-munching rattlesnakes! Then we can't do anything," cried Pam, collapsing onto a **WOODEN** bench.

We don't have proof!

But he's responsible!

"Well, I wouldn't say that. . . ." Paulina murmured.

"What do you mean?" Antonio asked her.

"I THINK I have a way to catch him and make him confess, but . . ."

"But what?" Violet pressed her.

Paulina turned toward Luz. "We'd need your help. But it would mean you'd have to face **Alvarez** in the fur, all alone. It could be dangerous. . . ."

I have a plan!

Paulina didn't have a chance to finish. **Luz** got it **RIGHT** away. "Don't worry about me. I'm not **afraid** to face that slimy sewer **RAT**!" she **EXCLAIMED**. "I'll do anything to help

Cocoa Loco. Tell me what you have in mind."

The FRIENDS gathered around Paulina as she outlined her plan.

"All right, sisters!" Pam exclaimed. "Now we just need to prepare our trap!"

TO CATCH A CROOK

The next day, **Luz** returned to the warehouse outside the city, ready to put Paulina's *plan* into action. This time she was alone. She waited impatiently for Pedro Alvarez to **APPEAR**.

A few hours earlier, the **mouselet** had left Alvarez a phone message saying she'd discovered his shady plans to sabotage

A TRAP FOR SABOTEURS!
STEP 1: LEAVE ALVAREZ A PHONE MESSAGE.

Cocoa Loco. She'd said she had **IMPORTANT** information about their rival business and suggested they meet at the warehouse alone.

As she waited, Luz paced back and forth like a rodent in a trap. She hoped that Alvarez would be curious enough to show up when he received her *invitation*. But the minutes crawled past, and she was getting discouraged. The **FUTURE** of Cocoa Loco was in her paws. . . .

Suddenly, a shadow fell over the room. Alvarez was standing there, blocking the **sunlight**.

"There you are!" Alvarez *hissed*. "What did that ᴘʜᴏɴᴇ ᴍᴇssᴀɢᴇ mean? Is this some kind of joke?"

Luz gathered her **COURAGE** before she replied, "No, it's no joke! I know all about your **SABOTAGE** of Cocoa Loco."

Alvarez burst out laughing. "Little mouselet, I don't know what you're talking about. But you'd better not **MAKE** accusations when you don't have proof. You'll get yourself in trouble. Haven't you thought about the consequences of accusing

your boss?" he demanded. "Your job is **VERY IMPORTANT** to you, if I'm not mistaken."

Luz was stunned. Alvarez was right. If she didn't succeed in her **MISSION**, she could lose her job and get Hector and Antonio into trouble.

Then the image of her *new friends*, the Thea Sisters, popped into her mind. They believed in her. She couldn't disappoint them!

Luz stared right into Alvarez's **EYES**, challenging him. "There won't be any consequences for me. I have proof of what I've said!" she said in the **bravest** tone she could muster.

For a moment, Alvarez looked **worried**. "What are you saying, you cheeky little mouselet? Proof of what?"

"Of your sabotage. You weren't as careful as you thought!" Luz declared.

Alvarez laughed again, but APPREHENSIVELY this time. "Oh, yeah? Go on, then, show me this proof! Where is it?" Alvarez loomed over Luz, forcing her to step back.

"I don't have it here," she replied. "Do you think I'm foolish enough to bring it here, so you could destroy it? No, I'm keeping it somewhere safe!"

Alvarez smirked angrily. "I don't believe a word you've said!"

"Really?" Luz replied. "Then you won't mind if I take the proof directly to the POLICE!"

SHOWDOWN!

Alvarez put his paws on his hips. "Silly mouse, you don't have a lick of proof, because I didn't do any of the things you said!" He tried to APPEAR confident, but his whiskers were twitching nervously.

"Really?" Luz said. "So it wasn't you who dumped fruit in the chocolate at Cocoa Loco? And released the pests on the plantation?"

"Of course not! You can't prove a thing!"

"Yes, I can!" Luz declared, trying to sound SURE of herself. She turned toward the ChocoMax SUV, which still had the empty boxes on board. "Someone saw this SUV near the Moreno cousins' plantation . . . and there are PHOTOS!"

Alvarez was startled. "What?"

"Yep!" Luz cried. "I've got photos, and I've hidden them far from here."

"Tell me where you put those pictures, you little **SNOOP**! You're sticking your snout into business that doesn't involve you!" shouted Alvarez.

"Business?! Don't you mean **sabotage**?" Luz cried.

Alvarez snorted. "Well, you could hardly expect a businessmouse like me to let a two-bit operation like **Cocoa Loco** win an important award like the Chocolate Cup!"

"I don't understand. . . ." Luz murmured, pretending to be surprised. "The **CHOCOLATE CUP**?! You did this just to keep the **Morenos** from winning the award?"

"Of course! Such a prestigious award is sure to bring investors to the winning **COMPANY** . . . and lots of big investors means lots of **money**!" Alvarez said scornfully. "The Morenos are like

That's horrible!

mouselings, playing around with their **old-fashioned** methods. They don't deserve to win! On the other paw, I'd know *exactly* what to do with that **PRIZE**! I'd cut down part of the forest and turn it into a **PLANTATION**. I'd use super-concentrated chemicals to triple my **PRODUCTION**, and —"

"But that's horrible!" Luz's protest shook him from his **DREAMS** of glory. "The **Morenos** make a quality product *and* respect the environment!"

"Not for long!" Alvarez growled. "My **ꙆNꙄＥＣＴ** friends are wreaking havoc on the Morenos' plantation as we squeak! And if that doesn't do the *trick*, I have a few other ideas that should. . . ."

"No!" Luz shouted. "I'll **STOP** you!"

"How?" the rodent sniggered. "With your little photographs? Now tell me where you put them! Come on, squeak up!"

Luz was so shaken by her boss's threats that she couldn't say a word.

"You don't want to tell me?" Alvarez pressed. "Well, I asked nicely. But I can also be not so nice. Luis! Diego! Get in here!"

SUDDENLY, two hulking rodents appeared in the doorway.

"Did you think you were clever, little mouselet? Well, I'm cleverer than you. I brought my helpers with me! Now we'll all go **FIND** those photos."

The two rodents strode up to Luz, ready to force her into **Alvarez's** SUV. That's when a squeak from outside shouted, "She might not stop you, but we will!"

HECTOR burst into the room, followed by Antonio, the Thea Sisters, and the local police.

Luz let out a *sigh* of relief. "Thank goodmouse! I was starting to think you'd **FORGOTTEN** me!"

Paulina ran over and took her paw. "We had to wait for Alvarez to confess everything before we came in."

"**What?!**" Alvarez cried. "But then . . . this was a trap?!"

"Of course!" Violet exclaimed. "We were just outside, along with the **police**, and we heard every word."

"Your story has more holes than a slice of Swiss, Alvarez!" Colette cried.

"B-but . . . the **PHOTOS**?!" the rodent stuttered, confused.

"The photos don't exist!" Luz explained.

"We didn't have any proof that we could use to **ACCUSE** you! So we had to make you talk."

Alvarez's fur turned **REDDER** than a tomato. "What!?" He was still gnashing his whiskers when the police `arrested` him and his accomplices and took them away.

Cocoa Loco was finally safe!

FRIENDS AGAIN

Hector reached for Luz's paw. "Thank you! What you did was amazing."

"Oh, it was no fur off my snout," she replied. "Actually, I was afraid I wouldn't be able to get Alvarez to confess."

Hector smiled. "You were **PERFECT.** He stepped right into our trap. And you saved our business!"

"I know you don't trust me, Hector," Luz said, "but I had to do something for Cocoa Loco. For Antonio, and for you."

"I was a complete cheesebrain to think that you could be **involved** in the sabotage," said Hector, shaking his snout. "I was MADDER than a cat with a bad case of fleas when you left so suddenly. I was **MAD** at you, and also at myself."

Luz **LOOKED** at him in surprise.

"I didn't understand why you left," Hector continued. "I should have done something to **KEEP YOU** with us. To be honest, I missed you a lot!"

Luz **BLUSHED**.

"I remember all the hours we spent talking about our plans for the **business**," the ratlet said. "And then the work to get the plantation and the warehouses running . . . It meant a lot, **LUZ**!"

The mouselet looked at him, **confused**.

"I'm asking you to come back to work with us, Luz. We need you! And please don't worry about your family: Now that business is going well, we can **help them**!" Hector **assured** her.

Luz looked at him with **EYES** shining

with tears. "You would really give me a *second chance*?"

"Of course! With you by our side, **Cocoa Loco** will be better than ever!"

Luz smiled. "I accept! There's nothing I want more than to work with you and

Antonio, and to be friends again."

Hector and Luz *hugged*. The Thea Sisters had to keep themselves from bursting into applause.

"At last we've figured everything out!" Nicky cried.

"Not everything . . ." Colette whispered.

"What do you mean?" Pam said, perplexed.

"I have a question for Luz, but I need to find the right moment!"

As the group HEADED for the van to drive back to Cocoa Loco, Colette pulled LUZ aside. "There's something I wanted to ask you. That day when we saw

I missed you!

you at Cocoa Loco, you had an **ENVELOPE** with you, right?"

Luz nodded. "Yes. I couldn't squeak directly to HECTOR, so I decided to put my suspicions into an anonymouse letter. I went to company headquarters to leave it for him. That's why you found me there!"

Colette's jaw dropped. "Your suspicions?! I was sure it was a love letter!"

Luz looked surprised. "Why would you think that?"

"Looks like your rodent's intuition isn't always spot-on, Coco!" Nicky said, giggling.

"I guess you're right," said Colette, shrugging.

Then, as she watched Luz approach Hector and take his PAW, she added, "Or maybe I was just a bit ahead of the times!"

THE AWARD

The next morning, the Thea Sisters were **ABUZZ** with excitement from the moment they woke up. Soon judges for the **CHOCOLATE CUP** award would inspect the plantations and the factory to decide if Cocoa Loco deserved to win!

"Keep calm and scurry on, mouselets!" Colette exclaimed.

"What's going on, Colette?" Pam asked, watching her friend **RUMMAGE** nervously through a closet overflowing with **clothes**.

"This is a fashion emergency! We need to hit some **shops**, stat!" Colette replied.

"Shopping? Has the cheese slipped off your cracker?" Pam said. "The **JUDGES** will be here any minute!"

"Exactly!" her friend cried. "And I have nothing to wear! An evening *gown* is too FORMAL, but my track suit is too casual. . . ."

"Oh, Coco!" Violet said. "I know you'll use your famouse CREATIVITY to mix a few styles together and come up with something fabumouse."

"MIX?" Colette breathed. "Vi, what a great idea!"

Colette dove back into her closet. A few minutes later, she emerged with the **PERFECT** outfit: a colorful printed blouse and a pair of sporty pants.

"It's just the right mix of elegance and comfort!" Colette exclaimed, twirling.

Soon the Thea Sisters stood at the factory entrance, waiting for HECTOR and Antonio to return from the plantations with the judges.

The judges seemed *pleasantly* surprised with the Cocoa Loco operation. They kept nodding as they chattered with the two cousins.

"Potatoes and soap to keep away insects!" exclaimed one. "**BRILLIANT!** You've rediscovered methods that are ancient but still effective."

The **JUDGE** next to him nodded. "Well done! It's not often you find a company that's so careful about the *environment*."

Antonio and Paulina exchanged a happy look: Thank goodmouse for Grandfather Imasu!

"Please, follow me," said Antonio. "I can't wait to show you our factory."

The Thea Sisters joined a group heading for the main workroom, where the equipment was WORKING at full speed. In the center of the room, a large, mysterious object covered with a green cloth stood on a platform.

"What's that over there?" asked one of the judges.

"A surprise for later," Antonio replied. "Now we'll show you the process we use to make our chocolate. Over there you can see the tanks with beans fresh from the plantations, ready for fermentation, and . . ."

"Look how *beautiful* they are!" Pam exclaimed, taking a bag of beans over to the JUDGES. But the bag was so heavy it **CRASHED** to the ground, scattering its contents at the judges' **paws**.

One judge lost her **BALANCE** on the little beans rolling underpaw. To slow down her fall, she grabbed the green cloth, which **came down** like a curtain, revealing . . .

Oops!

Uh-oh . . .

"Why . . . it's a **sun**!" exclaimed Colette.

"Made of **chocolate**!" Paulina continued, astonished.

Antonio helped the rodent get up. "It's a little **SURPRISE**," he explained.

"Little?!" Pam exclaimed. "**Crumbling chocolate chunks**, that thing must be five feet tall!"

Hector started to l$\overset{*}{au}$gh. "We wanted to

make the Cocoa Loco logo out of our best chocolate, the DARK BARK BAR!"

"The sun's rays represent the many rodents whose hard work and support helped make our dream come true," continued Antonio.

The judges exchanged a look of agreement. They didn't need to inspect anything else: The decision had been made!

"I think I squeak for everyone," began the rodent who had slipped on the cacao beans, "when I say that Cocoa Loco deserves our award this year! It's with great pleasure that we invite you to participate in the official presentation ceremony this evening. We'll be waiting for you onstage!"

After the judges had left, the Moreno cousins celebrated. They were more excited than a pack of mouselings at Ratty Potter World.

"Smokin' Swiss cheese, we did it!" shouted Antonio, hugging Paulina.

Colette, Nicky, Pam, and Violet high-fived. They were THRILLED that their adventure had such a happy ending!

We did it!

Hooray!

GOOD-BYE!

That evening, Colette didn't have the slightest doubt about what to wear: She selected her most *elegant* dress. In her fur she placed a clip in the shape of the **sun**, which she had made from the golden wrapper of a DARK BARK BAR.

"You look **gorgeous**!" Pam commented.

"Thanks! This seemed like the perfect occasion to indulge my passion for **fashion**," Colette replied, beaming.

The ceremony took place in a luxurious hotel. **Antonio** and **HECTOR** were waiting for them at the entrance.

Antonio came **FORWARD** and extended his paw to Paulina, WHISPERING, "You look marvemouse. Back on the playground all those years ago, I never imagined we'd have a **NIGHT** like this!"

"Me neither," replied Paulina. "But you and Hector deserve all this success!"

Congratulations!

Thank you so much!

They **ENTERED** a large hall where the presentation ceremony would take place and took their seats in the front row.

The **JUDGES** called the Moreno cousins to the stage and gave them their trophy: a plaque made of **solid gold**!

"For us, this is a dream come true!" Hector said into the microphone. "I would like to thank all those who helped us, especially **FIVE** very special mouselets who never give up: our FRIENDS the Thea Sisters!"

The entire hall **exploded** in applause. The mouselets beamed at one another and at their new friends.

After the ceremony, all the guests moved into a *fancy* salon, where a delicious-looking buffet of cheese and chocolate was waiting for them. Pam was first in line.

"Jumping gerbils, this is absolutely amazing!" she exclaimed.

At the center of the table was a large fountain gushing **pure chocolate**.

"After this trip, I might not be able to eat chocolate for a while!" Violet laughed.

"Well, we don't have such delicious fresh

chocolate at home. . . ." said Paulina, growing **SAD** at the thought of saying good-bye to their friends.

Antonio smiled. "Don't worry, **HECTOR** and I will make sure Mouseford receives a monthly shipment of **Cocoa Loco** products! That way you'll remember to come back and visit us soon."

Paulina **SMILED**. "Just tell us when, and we'll be here in two shakes of a rat's tail!"

The other Thea Sisters agreed with their friend. They cheered, "A friendship so sweet can never be forgotten!"

Don't miss these exciting Thea Sisters adventures!

Thea Stilton and the Dragon's Code

Thea Stilton and the Mountain of Fire

Thea Stilton and the Ghost of the Shipwreck

Thea Stilton and the Secret City

Thea Stilton and the Mystery in Paris

Thea Stilton and the Cherry Blossom Adventure

Thea Stilton and the Star Castaways

Thea Stilton: Big Trouble in the Big Apple

Thea Stilton and the Ice Treasure

Thea Stilton and the Secret of the Old Castle

Thea Stilton and the Blue Scarab Hunt

Thea Stilton and the Prince's Emerald

Thea Stilton and the Mystery on the Orient Express

Thea Stilton and the Dancing Shadows

Thea Stilton and the Legend of the Fire Flowers

Thea Stilton and the Spanish Dance Mission

Thea Stilton and the Journey to the Lion's Den

Thea Stilton and the Great Tulip Heist

Thea Stilton and the Chocolate Sabotage

Thea Stilton and the Missing Myth

Check out these very special editions featuring me and the Thea Sisters!

THE JOURNEY TO ATLANTIS

THE SECRET OF THE FAIRIES

THE SECRET OF THE SNOW

MEET
GERONIMO STILTONIX

He is a spacemouse — the Geronimo Stilton of a parallel universe! He is captain of the spaceship *MouseStar 1*. While flying through the cosmos, he visits distant planets and meets crazy aliens. His adventures are out of this world!

#1 Alien Escape

#2 You're Mine, Captain!

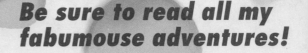

Be sure to read all my fabumouse adventures!

#1 Lost Treasure of the Emerald Eye

#2 The Curse of the Cheese Pyramid

#3 Cat and Mouse in a Haunted House

#4 I'm Too Fond of My Fur!

#5 Four Mice Deep in the Jungle

#6 Paws Off, Cheddarface!

#7 Red Pizzas for a Blue Count

#8 Attack of the Bandit Cats

#9 A Fabumouse Vacation for Geronimo

#10 All Because of a Cup of Coffee

#11 It's Halloween, You 'Fraidy Mouse!

#12 Merry Christmas, Geronimo!

#13 The Phantom of the Subway

#14 The Temple of the Ruby of Fire

#15 The Mona Mousa Code

#16 A Cheese-Colored Camper

#17 Watch Your Whiskers, Stilton!

#18 Shipwreck on the Pirate Islands

#19 My Name Is Stilton, Geronimo Stilton

#20 Surf's Up, Geronimo!

#21 The Wild, Wild West

#22 The Secret of Cacklefur Castle

A Christmas Tale

#23 Valentine's Day Disaster

#24 Field Trip to Niagara Falls

#25 The Search for Sunken Treasure

#26 The Mummy with No Name

#27 The Christmas Toy Factory

#28 Wedding Crasher

#29 Down and Out Down Under

#30 The Mouse Island Marathon

#31 The Mysterious Cheese Thief

Christmas Catastrophe

#32 Valley of the Giant Skeletons

#33 Geronimo and the Gold Medal Mystery

#34 Geronimo Stilton, Secret Agent

#35 A Very Merry Christmas

#36 Geronimo's Valentine

#37 The Race Across America

#38 A Fabumouse School Adventure

#39 Singing Sensation

#40 The Karate Mouse

#41 Mighty Mount Kilimanjaro

#42 Tho Peculiar Pumpkin Thief

#43 I'm Not a Supermouse!

#44 The Giant
Diamond Robbery

#45 Save the White
Whale!

#46 The Haunted
Castle

#47 Run for the Hills,
Geronimo!

#48 The Mystery in
Venice

#49 The Way of
the Samurai

#50 This Hotel Is
Haunted!

#51 The Enormouse
Pearl Heist

#52 Mouse in Space!

#53 Rumble in
the Jungle

#54 Get into Gear,
Stilton!

#55 The Golden
Statue Plot

#56 Flight of the
Red Bandit

The Hunt for the
Golden Book

#57 The Stinky
Cheese Vacation

#58 The Super
Chef Contest

**Don't miss my journey
through time!**

Be sure to read all my adventures in the Kingdom of Fantasy!

THE KINGDOM OF FANTASY

THE QUEST FOR PARADISE:
THE RETURN TO THE KINGDOM OF FANTASY

THE AMAZING VOYAGE:
THE THIRD ADVENTURE IN THE KINGDOM OF FANTASY

THE DRAGON PROPHECY:
THE FOURTH ADVENTURE IN THE KINGDOM OF FANTASY

THE VOLCANO OF FIRE:
THE FIFTH ADVENTURE IN THE KINGDOM OF FANTASY

THE SEARCH FOR TREASURE:
THE SIXTH ADVENTURE IN THE KINGDOM OF FANTASY

Meet
CREEPELLA VON CACKLEFUR

I, *Geronimo Stilton*, have a lot of mouse friends, but none as **spooky** as my friend CREEPELLA VON CACKLEFUR! She is an enchanting and MYSTERIOUS mouse with a pet bat named Bitewing. YIKES! I'm a real 'fraidy mouse, but even I think CREEPELLA and her family are AWFULLY fascinating. I can't wait for you to read all about CREEPELLA in these fa-mouse-ly funny and **spectacularly spooky** tales!

#1 The Thirteen Ghosts

#2 Meet Me in Horrorwood

#3 Ghost Pirate Treasure

#4 Return of the Vampire

#5 Fright Night

#6 Ride for Your Life!

Meet
GERONIMO STILTONOOT

He is a cavemouse — Geronimo Stilton's ancient ancestor! He runs the stone newspaper in the prehistoric village of Old Mouse City. From dealing with dinosaurs to dodging meteorites, his life in the Stone Age is full of adventure!

#1 The Stone of Fire

#2 Watch Your Tail!

#3 Help, I'm in Hot Lava!

#4 The Fast and the Frozen

#5 The Great Mouse Race

#6 Don't Wake the Dinosaur!

THANKS FOR READING, AND GOOD-BYE UNTIL OUR NEXT ADVENTURE!

Thea Sisters